THIS BOOK BELONGS TO:

_____

_____

To Lucy and Mary.

Printed by IngramSpark

www.chuwydesign.com
info@chuwy.es

Can I play?

GILBERTO MARISCAL

ILLUSTRATED BY CHUWY

WWW.CHUWYDESIGN.COM

That day little Mary woke Lucy up with great excitement.

It was her birthday!

The party was going to be in the backyard. Lucy and Mary prepared everything in the morning.

Ding dong! The doorbell! They were so nervous!
Lucy ran to open the door.
"Happy Birthday!" her friends sang.

Before going out to the garden, Lucy showed them her beautiful playroom.

"How nice!"
"So many toys!"

"Why don't we stay for a little while and play?"
her friends asked her.

But Lucy was not used to sharing her toys...

"Can I play with your teddy bear?" Paula asked.
"I'm sorry, but NO." Lucy said.

"Why not?" Paula insisted.

"Because mummy bear could get angry!"

So Paula left very upset.

"Will you lend me your scooter?" William asked.

"I'm sorry, but NO." Lucy said.

"Why not?" William insisted.

"Because if you do not have magical powers the wheels become square!"

So William left very sad.

"Can I play the drum?" Robert asked.

"I am sorry, but NO." Lucy said.

"Why not?" Robert insisted.

"Because evil mice will come and eat you!"

So Robert left very scared.

"What a beautiful dolls house! Can I borrow it?"
Alice asked.
"I am sorry, but NO." Lucy said.

"Why not?" Alice insisted.

"Because it is haunted and you could be locked up forever!"

Lucy made up stories more and more crazy
to not lend them her toys.

"Can I play with your horse?" Adele asked.

"I am sorry, but NO." Lucy said.

"Why not?" Adele insisted.

"Because my horse likes to escape out of the window to go to a forest full of ghosts!"

So Adele left terrified.

Her friends kept asking for toys, but Lucy always answered the same...

Lucy was left alone in the playroom.
With all her toys, but no friends to play with.

So she became very sad.

When she went to find her friends, she found them playing in the garden.

They seemed to be having a good time.

Lucy approached them timidly and asked:
"Can I play with you?"
"Of course! It is your birthday!"
her friends replied.

Gratefully, Lucy suggested bringing the toys out into the garden!

"Cool!" they all celebrated.

And they played...

When it was time for the cake, they blew out the candles together!

Lucy was very happy. The birthday party had been awesome!

Lucy received many gifts for her birhtday,
but there was a very special one...
... Rudolpha!

LUCY'S WORLD
BOOK SERIES

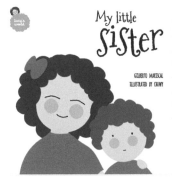

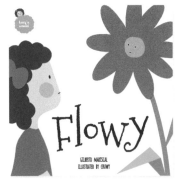

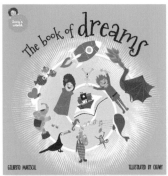

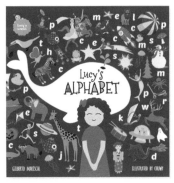

Lightning Source UK Ltd.
Milton Keynes UK
UKHW021849171220
375389UK00002B/7